Attack of
the Lizard King

Dinosaur Cove™

A Cretaceous Adventure

Dinosaur Cove™

Attack of the Lizard King

by
REX STONE

illustrated by
MIKE SPOOR

Series created by
Working Partners Ltd

OXFORD
UNIVERSITY PRESS

Special thanks to Jane Clarke

To the real Jamie Morgan, with love and kisses

OXFORD
UNIVERSITY PRESS

Great Clarendon Street, Oxford OX2 6DP
Oxford University Press is a department of the University of Oxford.
It furthers the University's objective of excellence in research, scholarship,
and education by publishing worldwide in

Oxford   New York

Auckland   Cape Town   Dar es Salaam   Hong Kong   Karachi
Kuala Lumpur   Madrid   Melbourne   Mexico City   Nairobi
New Delhi   Shanghai   Taipei   Toronto

With offices in

Argentina   Austria   Brazil   Chile   Czech Republic   France   Greece
Guatemala   Hungary   Italy   Japan   Poland   Portugal   Singapore
South Korea   Switzerland   Thailand   Turkey   Ukraine   Vietnam

Oxford is a registered trade mark of Oxford University Press
in the UK and in certain other countries

British Library Cataloguing in Publication Data

Data available

ISBN: 978-0-19-279365-2

1 3 5 7 9 10 8 6 4 2

Printed in Italy

Paper used in the production of this book is a natural,
recyclable product made from wood grown in sustainable forests
The manufacturing process conforms to the environmental
regulations of the country of origin

FACT FILE

➡ JAMIE HAS JUST MOVED FROM THE CITY TO LIVE IN THE LIGHTHOUSE IN DINOSAUR COVE. JAMIE'S DAD IS OPENING A DINOSAUR MUSEUM ON THE BOTTOM FLOOR OF THE LIGHTHOUSE. WHEN JAMIE GOES HUNTING FOR FOSSILS IN THE CRUMBLING CLIFFS ON THE BEACH HE MEETS A LOCAL BOY, TOM, AND THE TWO DISCOVER AN AMAZING SECRET: A WORLD WITH **REAL, LIVE DINOSAURS!** SOME DINOSAURS TURN OUT TO BE FRIENDLY, BUT OTHERS ARE FEROCIOUS AND... **HUNGRY!**

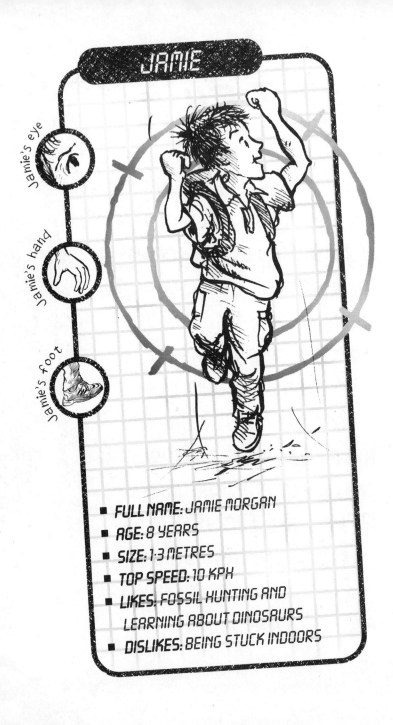

JAMIE

Jamie's eye

Jamie's hand

Jamie's foot

- **FULL NAME:** JAMIE MORGAN
- **AGE:** 8 YEARS
- **SIZE:** 1·3 METRES
- **TOP SPEED:** 10 KPH
- **LIKES:** FOSSIL HUNTING AND LEARNING ABOUT DINOSAURS
- **DISLIKES:** BEING STUCK INDOORS

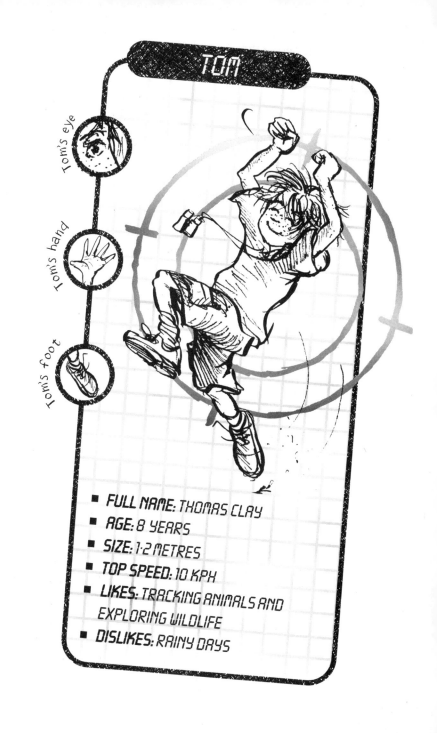

TOM

- Tom's eye
- Tom's hand
- Tom's foot

- **FULL NAME:** THOMAS CLAY
- **AGE:** 8 YEARS
- **SIZE:** 1·2 METRES
- **TOP SPEED:** 10 KPH
- **LIKES:** TRACKING ANIMALS AND EXPLORING WILDLIFE
- **DISLIKES:** RAINY DAYS

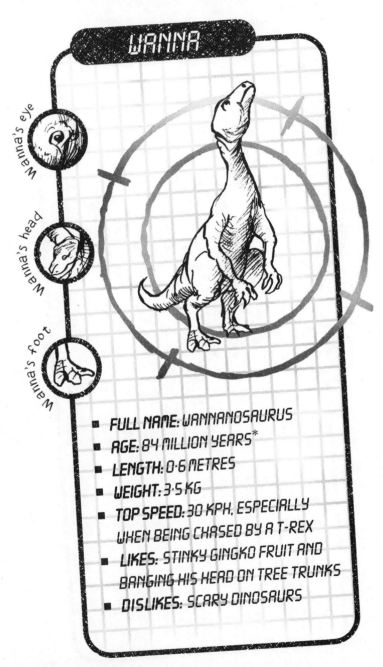

WANNA

Wanna's eye

Wanna's head

Wanna's foot

- FULL NAME: WANNANOSAURUS
- AGE: 84 MILLION YEARS*
- LENGTH: 0·6 METRES
- WEIGHT: 3·5 KG
- TOP SPEED: 30 KPH, ESPECIALLY WHEN BEING CHASED BY A T-REX
- LIKES: STINKY GINGKO FRUIT AND BANGING HIS HEAD ON TREE TRUNKS
- DISLIKES: SCARY DINOSAURS

*NOTE: SCIENTISTS CALL THIS PERIOD THE LATE CRETACEOUS

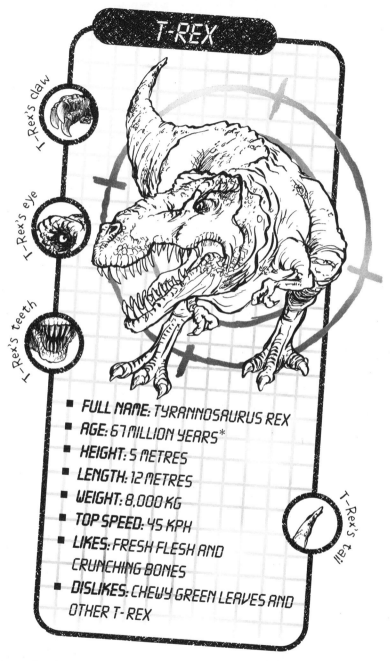

T-REX

T-Rex's claw

T-Rex's eye

T-Rex's teeth

- **FULL NAME:** TYRANNOSAURUS REX
- **AGE:** 67 MILLION YEARS*
- **HEIGHT:** 5 METRES
- **LENGTH:** 12 METRES
- **WEIGHT:** 8,000 KG
- **TOP SPEED:** 45 KPH
- **LIKES:** FRESH FLESH AND CRUNCHING BONES
- **DISLIKES:** CHEWY GREEN LEAVES AND OTHER T-REX

T-Rex's tail

*NOTE: SCIENTISTS CALL THIS PERIOD THE LATE CRETACEOUS

DINOSAUR COVE

Village

Marina

Sealight Head

Landslips where clay and fossils are

Muddy beach

DINO CAVE

High Tide beach line

Low tide beach line

Sea

Smuggler's Point

CHAPTER 1

'Dinosaur Cove!' Jamie ran to the cliff edge and looked down over the fence. 'This has got to be the best place on earth to find dinosaurs!'

His grandad's eyes twinkled. 'They're down there in the rocks,

that's for sure. Why don't you go and have a look?'

'Fossils, here I come!' Jamie said. 'See you later, Grandad.'

Jamie scrambled down the rocky path from the old lighthouse onto the sand. He turned away from the sea and ran straight up the beach, over pebbles and rocks, to the sludgy black mud nearest the foot of the cliff.

That was the place to find fossils. Jamie kept his eyes fixed on the muddy rocks and every so often he bent down to pick one up. They were crumbly and broke apart in his fingers, but none of them had a fossil inside. *Maybe I should try a bigger rock,* he thought.

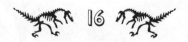

He spotted a large blue-grey rock with a crack down the middle and dumped his backpack on the mud beside it. He dug out his safety goggles and his fossil hammer and chisel. Then he set to work, angling the chisel into the crack and tapping it with his hammer. He tapped again. He tapped harder.

A stone chip pinged off Jamie's goggles as the rock split cleanly in two.

'Treasure!' Jamie said.

Sticking out of one half of the rock was a black spiral fossil with shiny gold ridges. He looked at it closely.

 17

It was about the length of his finger.
But when he tried to pick it out, it
was stuck fast in the rock.

*The Fossil Finder will tell me what
it is*, Jamie thought. He fished in
his backpack and took out his
favourite new gadget—a hand-held
computer. He flipped the lid and
the screen glowed with a picture of a
fossilized dinosaur footprint, then the
words: *'HAPPY HUNTING!'*

At the bottom of the screen, a cursor blinked. Jamie tapped *'FOSSIL SHELL'* on the small keypad, looked again at his fossil, and typed what it looked like: *'COILED ROPE'*. Then he pressed *'FIND'* and stared at the screen. A picture popped up. It looked just like the fossil in the blue-grey rock.

'AMMONITE,' Jamie read. *'A FOSSIL SHELL FROM A PREHISTORIC SEA CREATURE, COMMON IN ROCKS FROM DINOSAUR TIMES; CAN BE FORMED OF FOOL'S GOLD.'*

He flipped the lid shut.

'Well,' Jamie said to his discovery,

'I don't care that you're common, or that you're not real gold. You come from dinosaur times, and I'm the first person ever to see you. So you're still treasure to me!'

He pulled his goggles off, took out his new t-rex notebook and began to sketch his first Dinosaur Cove discovery.

He added in the squid-like tentacles and big eye that the creature would have had when it was alive.

Suddenly, an unfamiliar voice shouted,

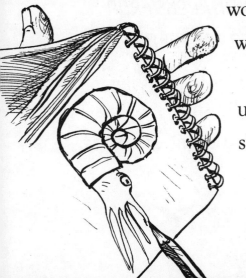

'BOO!'

A freckly face popped up from behind the rock. 'Gotcha! You didn't hear me coming, did you?' The boy stood up. His T-shirt and safari shorts were plastered in mud. 'Is that the new Fossil Finder?'

Jamie smiled and patted the lid. 'Latest software and everything.'

The boy pushed his curly red hair behind his sticky-out ears. 'I'm Tom Clay,' he said. 'I'm learning to track animals and I'm going to be a wildlife presenter on TV one day. Who are you?'

'Jamie Morgan,' said Jamie, 'I want to be a scientist.'

'You're new, aren't you?' Tom said.

Jamie nodded. 'I just moved here. Look! I found an ammonite.'

'Oh, ammonites,' said Tom, shrugging. 'You'll find loads of those around here.'

'I want to find a dinosaur bone,' Jamie told him. 'Dinosaurs are awesome!'

Tom looked at Jamie's notebook and laughed. 'T-rex rules!' He put his binoculars to his eyes. 'Sometimes I pretend I'm tracking dinosaurs . . . ' His binoculars flashed in the sunshine as he turned them on Jamie.

Tom grinned. 'Hey, do you want to know a secret about Dinosaur Cove?'

'You bet!' said Jamie.

'Then follow me. We have to be quick!' Tom set off across the beach.

Jamie stuffed his fossil-hunting gear into his backpack and ran after his new friend. 'Why are we hurrying?' Jamie asked.

'The path up the cliff gets cut off at high tide,' Tom said. 'So we'll have to get back before then.'

Tom led Jamie onto a narrow path up a cliff and at the highest point on the path, Jamie stopped to look at the view. He could see

Grandad fishing
down on the
beach.

'That's my
house,' Jamie told
Tom, pointing
to the tall white-
washed tower
at the top of
the cliffs on the
opposite side of
the beach.

Tom looked
surprised.
'The captain's
lighthouse?'

'The captain is my grandad,' Jamie explained. 'My dad moved us down here and he's turning the bottom floor into a dinosaur museum.'

'Cool!' said Tom. He turned to look at the huge pile of mossy boulders. 'We've got to get up there.'

'I love climbing!' Jamie said.

Together the boys clambered up the boulders. Once Jamie had hauled himself onto the huge stone at the top he asked, 'So, where's the big secret?'

'Right behind you,' Tom told him.

Jamie spun round. Behind the

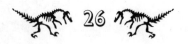

boulder and hidden from the bay was
the gaping mouth of a cave.

'A secret cave!' Jamie gasped.

CHAPTER 2

SEARCH:

'It's a smugglers' cave,' Tom told Jamie. 'It hasn't been used for a hundred years.'

Jamie stepped into the mouth of the dark cave and dug his hand into his backpack, pulling out his torch.

'This is where the smugglers stored
their booty,' Tom said. 'You can see
the marks from their lamps.'

Jamie flicked on his torch and shone
it over the pale rock walls. He could
make out sooty black streaks. Tom

took a few more steps into the cave and knocked on the back wall. 'It's a dead end.'

Jamie shone his torch over the floor and saw a spider with long, spindly legs. He followed it in the

beam as it skittered into the corner and then disappeared into a hole.

'It can't be a dead end,' Jamie said. 'Look!'

The hole began at the cave floor and went up to the height of his knees. It was wide at the bottom, but very narrow at the top.

'How did I miss that?' Tom said. 'I've been in here loads of times.'

'It's big enough to squeeze through.' Jamie knelt and pushed his backpack through the gap. 'I'm going in.' He wriggled through the gap, shining his torch into the darkness.

'Wait for me!' yelled Tom.

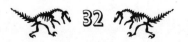

It was colder and pitch black inside the second chamber. Jamie shone his torch over the rock walls, ceiling, and floor. There was no sign of any soot from smugglers' lamps.

'We must be the first people to come in here for hundreds of years,' Tom murmured.

'Thousands of years!' said Jamie.

'Millions!' said Tom.

'Hey, what's this?' Jamie's torchlight fell on a scoop in the stone next to his feet. He knelt down and traced his finger around the clover-shaped indent. It looked just like the dinosaur footprint on his Fossil Finder.

'I think this could be a fossil,' Jamie announced, excitement tingling through him.

Jamie rummaged in his bag and flipped open the Fossil Finder. The display picture of a dinosaur footprint glowed in the darkness. 'Yes, it's a fossilized dinosaur footprint!'

'Wow,' Tom said, looking from the screen to the cave floor. 'Those are really rare!'

Jamie saw a second scoop at the edge of the beam of light. 'Look! There's another . . . and another . . . Five altogether. They go straight into that wall of rock.'

Jamie could hardly believe it. On his very first day exploring Dinosaur Cove, he had found the fossilized tracks of a dinosaur!

Jamie carefully placed his left foot into the first print. 'It's got the same size feet as me!' He swung his right foot into the next print. Jamie grinned at Tom, who was following behind him. 'We're tracking dinosaurs! Left foot.'

A crack of light appeared in the cave wall.

'Right foot . . . ' The light brightened as the crack widened. Jamie put his left foot forward to take another step and the crack of light got wider and brighter. He covered his eyes with his hands. When he put his foot down, the ground felt spongy.

Cautiously, he took his hands away from his eyes.

Jamie wasn't in the small dark chamber any more. He was in a sunny cave with a wall of stone behind him. The footprints were still

there—only now they weren't fossils.
They were fresh!

He took a step forward into the
new cave, and Tom appeared behind

him—right through
the wall of stone!
'Where are we?' Tom asked.
'I don't know,' Jamie said, looking
around at the strange new place.

Jamie walked out of the cave
and the ground squelched beneath
his feet. The area was thick with
trees and vines, so he couldn't see
very far.

'These trees are weird.' Jamie
pulled an apricot-like fruit from a
cluster hanging on a nearby branch.
It smelled horrible. 'Yuck! Dare you
to smell it, Tom.'

Tom took a huge sniff. 'Sick!' he
gasped. Then he grinned. 'Dare you
to take a bite.'

'No way!' said Jamie, shaking his
head.

The ground was slimed with the stinky orange outer pulp of the fruit that had fallen off the tree. Jamie picked up a fan-shaped leaf from the tree. 'You know, I think I've seen this somewhere before.'

He dug out the Fossil Finder and typed *'FAN-SHAPED LEAF'*. The next moment, pictures of leaves appeared on the screen. Jamie clicked on the one that looked the same as the leaf in his hand.

'GINGKO: A LIVING FOSSIL,' he read to Tom. *'STILL FOUND TODAY, BUT EVERYWHERE IN DINOSAUR TIMES; SOMETIMES KNOWN AS A STINK BOMB TREE.'*

'Too right,' said Tom. 'Let's get some fresh air!' He pushed aside a tangle of creepers. 'What's through here?'

'Wait for me!' Jamie hurriedly sealed a few gingko fruits into a plastic specimen bag, stuffed them and the Fossil Finder into his backpack, and then crashed through the undergrowth after Tom.

'Careful!' Tom shouted to him from up ahead.

The ground sloped steeply and Jamie tried to slow down, but his trainers were caked with slippery gingko pulp!

'I can't stop!' Jamie yelled as he tumbled towards the edge of a cliff.

Tom thrust out the end of a stick.
'Grab this, Jamie!' he shouted.

Jamie threw out his arm and
caught hold as one foot went over the
edge. He wobbled, and then steadied
himself. 'Thanks! That was close!'

Jamie stepped back from the
cliff edge and gazed at the landscape
in front of him. A canopy of grey
mist hung over a forest of brilliant

emerald green. The humid air throbbed with the whirring and buzzing of insects.

'Where is this?' he gasped. Among the trees, Jamie saw a beautiful blue lagoon and beyond that was an expanse of water. 'Is that Dinosaur Cove?'

'No way,' said Tom, looking through his binoculars. 'That's an ocean.'

Ark! Ark! Ark!

The sudden noise came out of the sky behind them and Jamie turned to see a scarlet-headed bird the size of a small aeroplane swooping towards them.

'Watch out!' he yelled to Tom.

They ducked as silver-grey leathery wings swept right over their heads. Tom followed the bird with his binoculars.

'It's flying over the jungle . . . it's settling on a tree by the lagoon,' he told Jamie. 'Take a look! It's huge!'

He thrust the binoculars at Jamie.

Jamie looked towards the lagoon and his jaw dropped open. He couldn't believe his eyes!

'What can you see?' Tom asked.

'I can see,' Jamie spoke carefully, 'two rhinos, but instead of one big horn, they have three. Which means,' he whispered, 'that they're not rhinos . . . they're triceratops!'

'What?' Tom said. 'Let me see!'

Jamie passed back the binoculars. 'You're right,' Tom said. 'And that huge bird is not a bird. It's a pterodactyl!'

The boys looked at each other in amazement.

'DINOSAURS!!'

they yelled together, punching the air.

'But how . . . ?' Tom stuttered.

'I don't know,' yelled Jamie. 'But we've got to get closer!'

'Over there,' said Tom. 'There's a slope down to the jungle.'

The boys scrambled and skidded down the hill, and soon their feet sank into the spongy jungle floor. Great conifers towered above them and huge ferns brushed damply against their legs as they passed. An enormous frill of purple and yellow spotted fungus caught Jamie's eye. It sprouted from a rotten tree stump.

'This is unreal!' Jamie said. But then, on the far side of the fungus, the ferns began to rustle.

Grunk.

'Did you hear that?' Jamie whispered.

'What?' Tom stood still.

The ferns swished. *Grunk.*

'That!' Jamie hissed. 'There's something there!'

Jamie and Tom ducked down behind the tree stump, and then slowly peeked out from behind the fungus.

The noises were coming from a plump scaly creature with a flat bony head and splotchy green-brown markings. It was standing on two strong legs, peering hopefully into a tree.

'It's a little dinosaur!' Jamie whispered.

 53

As they watched, the little dinosaur grabbed hold of the conifer with its claws, steadying itself by digging its long tail into the ground. Then it shook the tree as hard as its short arms would allow it to. The little dinosaur's tail twitched and it grunked softly to itself.

'He's thinking,' Tom murmured.

'He's so cool!' Jamie breathed.

The dinosaur took a few steps back. He lowered his bony head and charged straight at the tree.

Thwack!

The flat top of the dinosaur's head hit the tree trunk and the conifer shook.

'He's strong,' said Tom.

Thwack!

'Do you think he's dangerous?' Jamie asked.

'I'll look him up.' Tom pulled out the Fossil Finder from Jamie's backpack, and tapped in keywords:

'FLAT SKULL,' 'HEAD BUTT.'

'WAN-NA-NO-SAUR-US,' Tom read from the screen. *'A HERBIVORE.'*

'That means a plant eater,' added Jamie.

'USES ITS HARD SKULL TO DEFEND ITSELF AGAINST PREDATORS.'

As Tom slipped the Fossil Finder back into Jamie's bag, the little dinosaur took another run up and rammed the tree again.

'He thinks the tree's a predator!' Tom stood up, laughing.

At the sound of Tom's laughter, the little dinosaur cocked his head to one side. He turned and blinked mournfully at Tom.

'You've hurt his feelings,' Jamie said, standing up beside Tom.

'Sorry, Wanna,' Tom told the little dinosaur.

The wannanosaurus blinked at Tom and then at Jamie. He took three big steps away from the tree and shifted his weight from foot to foot.

'He's revving up,' said Jamie.

'Go, Wanna, go!' the boys shouted.

The wannanosaurus put his head down and hurtled towards the tree.

Thwack!

The tree wobbled.

Plunk!

A single pine cone dropped to the ground. The dinosaur stuffed it into his mouth and looked happily at the boys. Then he

wagged his tail and scurried off on his hind legs.

'Let's track him!' said Tom.

'Just a minute . . . ' Jamie carved a 'W' into the tree stump with his fossil hammer. 'So we remember where we met Wanna.'

'Now, which way did he go?' asked Jamie, as they clambered over the tree.

Tom looked around at the trampled plants. 'He disturbs the ferns as he walks on them,' Tom said. 'We can follow his trail.'

The little dinosaur's trail led to a small clearing and the boys found him standing on his hind legs,

munching a leaf. He turned towards
them and lowered his flat bony head.

'Uh oh,' said Tom. 'He might
charge us!'

'It's OK, Wanna. We're not
predators.' Jamie put his backpack
on the ground and took out his bag
of stinky gingko fruit. He rolled
one towards the wannanosaurus.
The dinosaur sniffed at the fruit
suspiciously.

'He can't possibly want to eat that,'
said Tom, holding his nose.

Wanna looked down his snout
at Tom, then he pinned the fruit
between his claws and sank his

60

teeth into it. He made grunking noises as stinky gingko juice dribbled down his chin.

'Yum yum!' Jamie grimaced as the dinosaur's long tongue slurped up every disgusting drop.

Wanna looked at Jamie. Then he looked at Jamie's backpack and wagged his tail.

Suddenly, the little dinosaur froze.

The jungle went still. Even the insects stopped buzzing. The ground trembled beneath their feet.

'Something's coming,' whispered Jamie. 'Something big . . .'

Thump! The ground shook. Wanna dashed behind the leafy tree.

Thump!

A stronger tremor shook the ground. Wanna peeped out from behind a branch and bobbed his head up and down.

In the distance,
wood was snapping and
cracking. The tremors
were getting stronger.

'Whatever it is, it's coming our
way,' Jamie said.

'Fast,' added Tom.

The boys looked at each other.

'We've got to get out of here!'
Jamie yelled.

'Which way?'

Suddenly, Jamie's bag was yanked

off his back. Jamie spun round and saw Wanna charging off into the jungle, clutching it in his mouth.

'Wanna!' Jamie sprinted after him, Tom close behind.

The little dinosaur skidded to a halt by a shallow stream. He turned and looked Jamie in the eyes. Then he jerked his head towards the stream and plunged in.

The ground shook again.

'Wanna's leading us to safety!' Jamie shouted, jumping into the stream after him.

'Clever!' Tom panted. 'The water will mask our scent.'

Wanna led them up the stream to where it trickled through a jumble of huge rounded rocks. He glanced back and leaped out of the water.

Jamie and Tom followed, stumbling and splashing. They scrambled onto the rocks and stood, dripping.

'Where's he gone?' Jamie said.

RAAAR!

Something crashed through the trees behind them. Jamie whirled round and lost his footing on the wet stone.

Tom threw out his hand, but when Jamie grabbed it both boys toppled

and slid down
between two rocks.
Jamie landed with
a thud and found
himself staring into a
reptilian face.

Grunk!

Wanna greeted
Jamie and Tom
with slobbery
licks, and Jamie
was happy to see his
backpack again.

'Are we safe?' Jamie
whispered. 'Has that
thing chasing us gone?'

The boys listened.

'I think so!' Tom breathed.

Thud!

The rocks shook.

'It's here!' Tom whispered.

Jamie peered up through the gap above his head. Instead of the trees of the jungle, he saw a dark slimy hole.

Suddenly, a blast of slime flew from the hole and splattered Jamie's face.

'*Aargh!*' Jamie wiped his face. 'I think that's its nose.'

The creature lifted its head and roared.

 69

RAAAR!

The sound rumbled
around the rocks.

Jamie could
see its jaws. Slithers
of rotting flesh dangled
from its fangs.

'Ugh! Bad breath!' Jamie gagged.
'Worse than stinky gingko fruit.'

'It doesn't look friendly,' Tom said.
'W-what is it?'

An enormous yellow eye, rimmed
with bright red scales, studied Jamie
through the gap in the rocks.

'D-don't n-need the F-Fossil

Finder,' Jamie stammered. 'It's a

T-T-T-REX!'

The eye disappeared.

'We're in trouble!' Jamie breathed.

'*Serious* trouble,' Tom said.

Suddenly, a long claw stabbed down into the crevice.

'Watch out!' Jamie yelled. He pulled

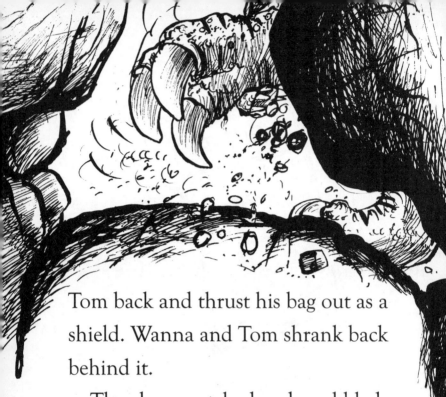

Tom back and thrust his bag out as a shield. Wanna and Tom shrank back behind it.

The claw scratched and scrabbled around the gap in the rocks.

'It can't get us!' Tom whispered. 'Its arms are too short.'

'Maybe it will go away now,' Jamie said. But the huge unblinking eye of the t-rex reappeared.

Wanna trembled.

'If I had a stick,' Tom muttered.
'I'd poke it in the eye!'

'There must be something we can use.' Jamie groped in his backpack. 'Let's see how it likes this.' Jamie pulled out his torch and aimed it at the t-rex's eye. He flicked it on.

RAAAR!

The eye vanished. Cautiously, Jamie poked his head out of the crevice. The t-rex was stomping away into the jungle.

'Whew!' Jamie said. 'I think we're safe.'

75

The boys gave each other a high five.

'Now, let's get out of here,' Tom said. 'Before it comes back!'

The boys and the little dinosaur climbed out of the crevice, and Wanna took the lead again, heading further downstream. 'Did you see that thing's teeth?' Jamie muttered as they splashed after their new dinosaur friend. 'That t-rex could rip us to shreds!'

'And eat us alive, bit by bit!' Tom shuddered.

Gradually, the stream grew wider and the trees on either side began to

thin out. Soon, the boys had come to the edge of the blue lagoon that they had seen earlier from Gingko Hill. Wanna stopped near a large rock and began to munch on a leafy bush.

'We've come a long way from the cave,' Tom said. 'And there's a t-rex out to get us. How are we ever going to get back home?'

'I-I don't know . . . ' Jamie gazed over the sparkling blue water. Behind them, something started squawking.

The boys whirled round. The squawks were coming from the yellow beaks of batlike reptiles in the palm tree. The creatures looked like

badly folded brown umbrellas, gripping the palm fronds with their scaly feet and the clawed fingers on their wings.

'They must be another type of pterodactyl,' Tom decided.

Just then, the pterodactyls launched themselves into the air, squawking and flapping their wings.

'What's up with them?' Tom asked as the bird-like creatures flew away.

The
lagoon fell
silent. The only
sound was the
water gently
lapping the
shore. Then the ground began to
shake.

'Uh oh,' Jamie and Tom said
together.

'T-REX!'

CHAPTER 6

The boys turned to see the t-rex
spring out of the jungle, sending
up a spray of sand. Its green scales
rippled in the sunshine as it
scanned the beach.

Then, it saw them.

81

RAAAR!

The t-rex lowered its head. The red crests over its eyes flashed as it stomped towards them.

'We're t-rex food,' moaned Tom.

Then, suddenly, there was a sound of breaking branches behind them. The t-rex's head snapped up and it stared at the edge of the jungle.

Turning round slowly, Jamie saw a second t-rex crash out of the trees onto the beach.

'Oh no!' said Tom.

It was as big as the first, but darker, with black stripes. And it was advancing on them.

'Watch out!' Jamie rolled out of the way of a huge foot as the first t-rex stomped to meet the other t-rex.

Tom
ducked
as its tail
swept over
his head.
The boys watched
as the first t-rex hurled
itself at the newcomer.
'They're not after us!' he breathed.
'Maybe they're fighting over
territory,' Tom guessed.
The first t-rex sank its jaws into
the other's throat. The dark t-rex

screeched and writhed and thrashed its tail. Then it broke free, and sprang onto the first t-rex's back. It hung on, biting its neck.

'Let's get out of here! Run!' Jamie dragged Tom towards the trees. Wanna bounded after them.

Gradually, the snarls and roars of the t-rex battle faded into the jungle sounds.

'We're lost, aren't we?' Tom sat down on the ground and put his head in his hands. 'How are we going to get back?'

Grunk . . . grunk . . . grunk . . .

Wanna darted off into the trees.

'Maybe we could follow Wanna?' Jamie said. 'It's our best chance.'

After a moment, they were back at a stream. 'Is this the same stream as before?' Jamie wondered.

Next, Wanna led them down a jumble of rounded rocks.

'That's where we hid from the t-rex!' Tom grinned.

They passed the purple and yellow-spotted fungus and Jamie bent down and saw the 'W' on the tree stump. 'The Wanna tree!' he grinned.

Then they climbed the slope through the gingko trees and, finally,

they were standing in the mouth of
the cave.

'That's how we got here!' Jamie
pointed to the fresh dinosaur footprint
by the solid rock wall.

Wanna stood next to it, and wagged
his tail. Then he stepped away, leaving
two more identical footprints, but this
time facing the rock.

'They're your footprints!' Jamie gasped.

Wanna blinked at him, turned,
and scurried into a pile of leaves and
twigs in the corner of the cave.

'That's Wanna's nest!' Jamie took
out the last gingko fruit from his
backpack.

'This is for you, Wanna,' he said, putting it on the ground. 'Thank you for helping us.' Wanna's snout poked out of his nest. He nosed the fruit back to Jamie.

'I think he wants you to have it,' Tom said.

'OK, Wanna,' said Jamie, picking it up. 'I'll put it in Dad's museum,' he told Tom, screwing up his nose and smiling.

Tom was gazing at the rock with a puzzled expression on his face. 'We stepped forward to go back in time, so maybe we have to step backwards to go forward in time,' he guessed.

Jamie nodded. 'I hope it works!'

Tom turned his back to the rock face. Then he placed his right foot in Wanna's print and stepped back with his left. There was a flash of light and Jamie found himself alone with Wanna.

'It worked!' Jamie said to Wanna. 'That means we can come back and see you again!'

He patted the little dinosaur on the snout. Wanna licked Jamie's hand, then curled up in his nest.

'Goodbye, Wanna!' Jamie held the gingko fruit in one hand and his torch in the other. As he stepped back through the blaze of light, he felt the ground turn to stone beneath his feet. Then, he was back in the cave with Tom.

Jamie felt the gingko fruit in his hand soften. In the torch beam, he watched it shrivel and crumble to dust.

'We can't bring anything back,' he told Tom, letting the dust trickle between his fingers.

'It's just as well,' Tom said. 'That thing stank.'

The boys squeezed through the hole in the rock, scrambled down the boulders, and hurried down the cliff path onto the beach. Jamie's grandad was packing up his fishing gear.

He smiled at the boys as he reeled in his fishing line.

'Did you find any dinosaurs?' he asked them.

Jamie winked at Tom. 'We found a brilliant cave, didn't we, Tom?'

'Awesome!' agreed Tom. 'Let's explore it some more tomorrow!'

'Great idea!' said Jamie, hoisting up his backpack, and turning to Grandad. 'If that's OK with you and Dad?'

'Just as long as you're not getting into any scrapes . . . ' Grandad's eyes twinkled as he slung his fishing rod over his shoulder and picked up his bucket of fish.

'See you tomorrow, Tom?' Jamie said to his new friend.

'Sure thing!' Tom said as he waved goodbye.

Jamie and Grandad walked back up the path to the old lighthouse. Grandad asked, 'You think you'll like living round here then?'

'Definitely!' said Jamie with a grin. 'I can't wait to explore more of Dinosaur Cove!'

DINOSAUR WORLD

----- BOYS' ROUTE

Jungle

Misty Lagoon

White Ocean

98

Far Away Mountains

Crashing
Rock
Falls

Great Plains

Fang
Rock

Gingko
Hill

GLOSSARY

Ammonite (am-on-ite) – an extinct animal with octopus-like legs and often a spiral-shaped shell that lived in the ocean.

Conifer – cone-bearing trees such as pines or cedars.

Fossil – the remains or imprint of plants or animals found in rocks. They help scientists unravel the mysteries of prehistoric times.

Fossil Finder – hand-held computer filled with dinosaur facts.

Gingko (gink-oh) – a tree native to China called a 'living fossil' because fossils of it have been found dating back millions of years, yet they are still around today. Also known as the stink bomb tree because of its smelly apricot-like fruit.

Herbivore – an animal that only eats plants; a vegetarian.

Lagoon – a body of water, like a lake, that is separated from a larger body of water, like an ocean, by a barrier of coral or sand.

Pterodactyl (ter-oh-dak-til) – a flying prehistoric reptile which could be as small as a bird or as large as an aeroplane.

Triceratops (t-tops) (try-serra-tops) – a three-horned, plant-eating dinosaur which looks like a rhinoceros.

Tyrannosaurus Rex (t-rex) (ti-ran-oh-sor-us rex) – a meat-eating dinosaur with a huge tail, two strong legs but two tiny arms. T-Rex was one of the biggest and scariest dinosaurs.

Wannanosaurus (wah-nan-oh-sor-us) – a dinosaur that only ate plants and used its hard, flat skull to defend itself. Named after the place it was discovered: Wannano in China.

Look out!
Here I come . . .

Turn the page
to read the
first chapter of the
next adventure in the

Dinosaur Cove™

series:

Charge of the
Three-Horned Monster

Jamie Morgan sprinted along the
pebbly beach of Dinosaur Cove to
meet his new best friend.

'Have you got everything?' asked
Tom Clay, jumping off the rock
he was standing on. 'I brought my
binoculars and my compass.'

Jamie took off his backpack and rummaged inside for his fossil hunting equipment. 'I've got my pocket knife, my notebook, and the Fossil Finder.' Jamie's brand new hand-held computer had all sorts of prehistoric information at the touch of a few buttons. 'I brought some sandwiches, too,' Jamie said. 'Cheese and Grandad's home-made pickle. It'll blow your head off!'

'I can't wait to get back to our cave,' Tom said, hopping from one foot to another.

'You mean you can't wait to get back to the dinosaurs!' Jamie said, as the two friends hurried down the beach. Jamie had met Tom for the first time yesterday and together they had discovered Dinosaur Cove's biggest secret: an amazing world of living dinosaurs! First, Jamie had found a set of fossilized dinosaur footprints, and then the footprints had transported them to a place where dinosaurs still roamed the earth.

'It's hard keeping something so big a secret,' Tom confessed. 'My big brother kept asking me what I did yesterday.'

'I know!' Jamie replied. 'My dad got a huge triceratops skull fossil for the museum this morning, and I kept thinking about the real triceratops we saw yesterday.'

Jamie and his dad had moved in with his grandad to the old lighthouse on the cliffs and Jamie's dad planned to open a dinosaur museum on the ground floor. Jamie's dad knew more about dinosaurs than anyone, but he didn't know the colours of a t-rex like Jamie and Tom did!

'I forgot to tell you!' panted Jamie, as they scrambled up the steep path towards their secret cave. 'I brought some coloured pencils with me. I thought we could make a map of Dino World in my notebook.'

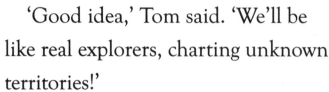

'Good idea,' Tom said. 'We'll be like real explorers, charting unknown territories!'

'And seeing lots of dinosaurs!'

They reached the tall stack of boulders that led to their secret cave, and climbed up using cracks in the rock. From the top of the boulders, Jamie could see his grandad fishing for lobster out in the cove.

Jamie quickly
slipped into the
dark cave, but
Tom paused at the
hidden entrance.
'What if Dino
World's not there?'
he asked. 'What if we
dreamt it?'

Jamie laughed, and the sound
echoed around the cave. 'No way!
That t-rex we met was definitely
real!' With a shiver of excitement he
turned on his torch and shone it into
the far corner. The beam picked out
the small gap in the cave wall.

Jamie took off his backpack and crawled through on his belly into the second chamber which was narrower and pitch dark. Jamie and Tom suspected they were the only people ever to have been in this place.

Jamie flashed his torch over the stone floor. 'Here are the fossilized dinosaur footprints we found yesterday.'

'The best fossil anyone has ever found!' Tom said. The footprints had somehow transported the boys to Dino World.

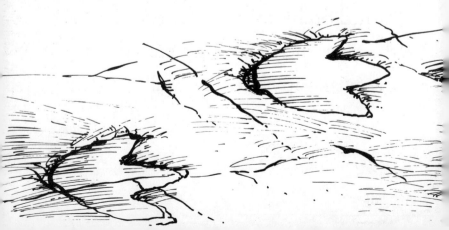

Tom stepped into the first clover-shaped indent in the cave floor. 'Here goes!' He placed his foot carefully into each footprint, walking in the dinosaur tracks.

Jamie stuck close behind him and counted every step. 'One . . . two . . . three . . . four . . . FIVE!'

In an instant, the cold, damp cave was gone and Jamie and Tom were standing in a bright sunny cave and staring out at giant, sun-dappled trees.

The air was hot and humid and they could hear the heavy drone of insects. They ran out on to the damp squelchy ground of Dino World.

'We're back in the jungle,' said Jamie happily. 'We're on Gingko Hill.'

'This is so cool!' said Tom, looking eagerly around.

Jamie laughed. 'Boiling, you mean!' He picked a large leaf off the ground and fanned himself. Suddenly he stopped. 'What was that?'

The boys listened hard. From somewhere in the steaming jungle they could hear scuffling—and it was getting nearer.

'Something's coming!' warned Tom.

Just then, a plump, scaly little creature with a flat, bony head burst out from a clump of ferns. It scuttled along on its stumpy hind legs and hurled itself at Jamie, knocking him flat on his back.

Grunk! Grunk! Grunk!

'It's Wanna!' exclaimed Tom in relief.

Jamie and Tom had met the wannanosaurus on their first visit to Dino World, and the Fossil Finder had said that it was pronounced 'wah-nan-oh-sor-us'. Wanna had helped them when the t-rex was after them and turned out to be a true friend.

'Stop licking, Wanna!' panted Jamie, trying to push him off. 'Your tongue's like sandpaper.'

Tom reached up to a nearby gingko tree and picked a handful of the small, foul-smelling fruit. He held one out. 'Have a stink-o bomb, Wanna. Your favourite!'

Wanna bounded over and greedily gobbled it up as Jamie staggered to his feet. Tom gave him one more and then quickly tossed a few more pieces of the fruit to Jamie, who hid them in his backpack.

'Let's start mapping!' said Tom.

Wanna sniffed the bag as Jamie dug around and pulled out his notebook and coloured pencils. 'We're here,' he said, drawing Gingko Hill in the middle of the page.

'Yesterday we found the ocean and the lagoon in the west.' He sketched them in.

Tom checked the compass. 'So let's head north today.'

'Great,' said Jamie. 'Come on, Wanna! We're going exploring.'

Wanna wagged his tail and trotted happily alongside the boys. They scrambled through ferns and creepers and squelched among slimy giant toadstools.

At last they came to a break in the trees and peered through. Below was the dense tangle of the jungle and beyond that vast grassy plains

with a wide river
snaking through towards
their hill.

'Look at those far away
mountains,' said Tom,
scanning the horizon

with the binoculars. 'They're so
high their peaks are hidden in the
clouds.'

'Far Away Mountains—that's a
good name!' said Jamie, and scribbled
it down on the map.

Then Jamie took the binoculars and scanned the plains, and what he saw made him gasp. There were about fifteen strange-looking houses made of orange earth sitting near a curve in the river.

'What is it?' Tom asked.

'I don't know,' Jamie replied. 'I think . . . I think there's a village!'

Join Jamie and Tom
in **Dino World**
with the

Dinosaur Cove ™

CRETACEOUS
SURVIVAL GUIDE

Turn the page for a taster

of all the **awesome**

things to do . . .

Create!

MRKE YOUR OWN EDIBLE DINO POO!

YOU WILL NEED:

- 100g plain chocolate
- 50g margarine
- 2 tablespoons golden syrup
- 150g plain digestive biscuits

Don't forget to ask a grown-up to help melt the chocolate!

1 Put the biscuits in a large freezer bag and tie the bag shut. Using a rolling pin, bash the biscuits into crumbs.

2 Break up the chocolate into pieces and put them in a saucepan. Heat the pan on a low temperature until the chocolate has melted.

3 Stir the margarine and syrup into the melted chocolate.

4 Take the saucepan off the heat. Pour the biscuit crumbs into the chocolate mixture and stir together.

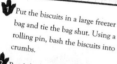

36

37

Play!

WHICH CRETRCEOUS DINO RRE YOU?

START
Do you walk on two legs or four legs?

Two legs / Four legs

Super speedy or supremely strong?

Super speedy or supremely strong?

Strong / Speedy

Speedy / Strong

Carnivore or herbivore?

Up high or down low?

Protected by horns or bony armour?

Hunt on land or in the air?

Land / Air

Carnivore / Herbivore

Down low / Up high

Horns / Bony armour

T-Rex   Quetzalcoatlus   Velociraptor   Wannanosaurus

Bagaceratops   Edmontosaurus   Triceratops   Ankylosaurus

Discover!

DINOSAUR DIMENSIONS
SCALE

Quetzalcoatlus
Height (when standing): 6m
Wing span: 12m

Jamie and Tom
Height: 1.3m and 1.2m

Velociraptor
Height: 0.75m
Length: 2m

Ankylosaurus
Height: 2m
Length: 11m

Triceratops
Height: 3m
Length: 10m

Edmontosaurus
Height: 3m
Length: 12m

Tyrannosaurus Rex
Height: 5m
Length: 12m

24   25

Explore!

T-REX: THE LIZARD KING

Tyrannosaurus Rex was a carnivore that ate all sorts of other creatures, from small dinosaurs like velociraptors to large ones like edmontosaurs. Palaeontologists think the t-rex was probably a scavenger as well as a hunter, eating up the remains of creatures that had already died. With chisel-shaped teeth at the front and huge teeth with knife-like serrated edges filling the rest of its mouth, the t-rex was a fearsome predator. The biggest t-rex skull ever found is 150cm long and was discovered in the 1960s. The biggest and best preserved whole t-rex skeleton is in the Field Museum of Natural History in Chicago. Its name is FMNH PR 2081, but its nickname is Sue.

We found out that competition for food was fierce in the Cretaceous period when we ran into not one but **two** t-rexes! We'd only just managed to escape one dino's snapping jaws when we stumbled into a battle between two of the massive lizard kings.